BILLIONAIRE'S SEXY HACKER

GAY ROMANCE

GAY BILLIONAIRES
BOOK TWO

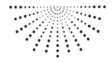

DILLON HART

CHAPTER ONE

SULLY

I'm holding the last potential candidate's resume in my hand, and glance once again over the details which I've already committed to memory. My co-interviewer and I are in my office, taking a quick break between meetings.

The final interview was slated to start five minutes ago.

As CEO and majority owner of Fuller Securities Corp, I rarely take an active role in the interview process itself. But this role is so high profile and important, I've decided to handle recruitment personally.

The stakes are too high. There's too much on the line.

It's good technique to keep candidates waiting, to see if they can handle a little extra pressure. The weak ones really sweat it out after being told upon arrival that the CEO himself is going to run the interview.

But this candidate though... I'm fairly sure he's never been under such pressure in his entire life.

"You sure about this one, boss?" Gareth Holdt asks, as if reading my mind. My company's head of talent management shifts in his seat, looking down at the resume in front of him again.

I grunt in response.

"I mean sure, he's done the research, got a doctorate in security software systems - but can he handle real life? This contract - "

I rise quickly, towering over Gareth at six foot four, silencing him with a glare.

"Don't tell me about the contract," I growl. "Why do you think I'm spending my precious time interviewing a twenty-something graduate? And as for this Williams? I'll go see what he's made of."

Marching from the room, I leave Gareth scurrying along behind me. Heading for the interview room, I gesture for Gareth to go collect Mister Williams from reception.

Settling into the large desk opposite the door, I command the room from a central spot. My posture is ramrod straight, hands folded over one another in front of me, my practiced expression that of irritated impatience.

A minute or so later the door opens, and a boyish figure enters, his eyes sweeping the room before widening as they settle on me.

Big, hazel brown eyes flash with intelligence behind fashionable, thick framed glasses. Long dark hair, tied smartly into a short ponytail at the base of his neck, reveals an angular, birdlike face. He's obviously very slender, I can tell by the fitted suit he's wearing. He barely looks like he's reached adulthood but his suit is of obviously high quality.

I keep my face expressionless as I study him for a moment, something that comes naturally after years of military training and service.

He's what I was expecting, but something a little more too. Geeky, with that flash of high intelligence in his eyes, that mysterious half-smile…

And he's damn hot. That face, those angles. Those eyes…

I half rise and hold out a hand, as Gareth enters the room behind him. He studies my hand for a moment, as if in surprise, before offering his. For a second, my huge hand envelops his smaller, softer one and a surge of something like protectiveness washes over me.

I glance at Gareth, who taps his watch and jerks his thumb over his shoulder. He has a senior management presentation to attend. Dipping my chin, I let him know I'll handle this and he quickly leaves.

"Sully Fuller. Majority shareholder and CEO. Mister Williams?"

He starts to turn red as I grasp my hand with his, the skin of his slender fingers soft and warm. A thrill of pleasure tingles on my skin at his touch.

"A pleasure to meet you, Mr. Fuller. Please, call me Marek," he replies softly.

I gesture for him to sit, and then take a seat myself once he does.

"So, Marek. What do you know about the company?" I ask.

He smiles knowingly, instantly looking more confident.

"I've done a little research," he says. "You created Fuller Securities after injury forced early retirement from the marines. The company started out as a private security firm, offering physical security, before expanding to the current corporation, where I believe you have branched out into defense and alarms systems, and now cybersecurity."

I nod, impressed.

"Very good. So, I'm guessing you know where you'll come in. After a... rather drawn out bidding process, we have been chosen to provide cybersecurity backup and testing for a well-known arms and military systems developer. The details of which I can't fully disclose, for now," I say in a matter-of-fact tone.

"Suffice to say that you'll be working on testing the robustness of a brand new and complex security system, which will be used to protect our client's considerable data interests," I continue. "Like I said, the system is brand new. Developed in house by a joint venture between our best tech guys, and their security systems experts. And so…"

I trail off, and gesture expansively with my hands, inviting him to chime in.

"You need to see if it works as well as you hope it does," he responds with a knowing nod.

I point a finger at him, and smile briefly at his quick wit.

"Exactly. And that's where you come in. Well, that's if we hire you, of course," I say.

He smiles nervously and flushes a little, doing his best to thaw my icy manner, in my mind at least.

You'll have to do better than that. Maybe if you started unbuttoning that shirt...

I push the sudden and unexpected desires from my thoughts, and frown at him.

"So, tell me a little about yourself," I say, and he jumps a little at the sudden question.

"Ah, well, there's not much to say. I recently completed my doctorate in computer coding and systems, specializing in public data security systems," he glances away for a moment, before looking back at me. "And I'm not going to lie. I love computers. Coding, developing software, simulated hacking, gaming…"

"Simulated hacking?" I ask, interrupting him.

He nods in response.

"That's right. There was a group of us at university, the, uh, computer coding geeks, if you like. We would challenge each other as part of our research. We would take it in turns for one of us to develop a simulated defense system on the university servers, and the rest of us would race to hack it."

He smiles as he talks, obviously enjoying the memory.

"And whoever came last would buy the first two rounds of drinks that Friday." He flushes again, as if regretting his admission of having a little fun.

I grunt, impressed and slightly amused. But my gut twists a little at his words, and the look in his eyes, a look of… guilt? Shame perhaps? Something doesn't seem to add up, but I decide not to press him further.

"So you're telling me that if I hire you, you'd actually enjoy the work?" I say, amused. I glance down at the papers in front of me. "I'm not sure that's in the job description."

Marek laughs nervously at my lame joke, and I can't help but smile at the sound. Our eyes meet as silence descends in the room, and something passes between us.

An understanding? Attraction? No, get a hold of yourself Sully. He's just a kid and you don't even know for sure if he's into men, let alone men old enough to be his father.

"Here's the deal," I continue. "I'll be straight with you. This contract is the most valuable we've had here at Fuller Corp for a long time. It's important that we get this right. But, it's equally important we protect our client's interests, too."

"I understand," he interjects, nodding seriously.

"Good," I reply. "Which is why you'll be sworn to secrecy, in the form of a series of non-disclosure agreements, all of which are legally binding. Everyone at the company has had to sign them, so it's nothing unusual. But suffice to say, this company is not one you want as an enemy."

His eyes widen, more with excitement than fear. I find myself impressed, yet again.

I study his pretty boy face for a moment, the thoughtful pout on his full lips, and the soft skin of his immaculate white cheeks unmarred by stubble. The more I look at him, the more ethereal he becomes, almost as if I'm falling under the effect of some sort of impish spell.

I suppress a sigh of wistful desire, and look him in the eye once again.

"So, as I hope you can see, this is something rather serious for me and my company, and equally so for our client. I understand this might be a bit… daunting for you, but I've got a good feeling about you, Marek. I think you might just be the one for the job."

He grins broadly and sits up straight on his chair, seemingly unaware that the movement serves to accentuate the outline of his slender white neck, stretching impossibly long from underneath the thin material of his dress shirt. He looks like some kind of Renaissance painting come to life.

"I would understand if you think this role is too much for you," I add. "But assuming it isn't, well, why should we hire you?"

His eyes widen in surprise, and he opens his mouth to speak, but he's stunned to silence for a moment.

Oh, you didn't think it was going to be that easy, did you? Let's see how fast you can think on your feet.

CHAPTER TWO

MAREK

Just when I thought I had nailed this interview, he fires that one at me. I can tell he's ex-military, his expression is unreadable, unknown thoughts passing back and forth between those incredibly handsome, light blue eyes of his as they sparkle with intelligence.

I open my mouth to speak, but no words come out.

"Why should you hire me?" I reply slowly, buying myself some time to think.

I've already told you. I'm perfect for the damn job. Oh, you're enjoying this, aren't you? If only you weren't so damn hot, it would make me being pissed off so much easier.

"I may be young, and seemingly inexperienced," I say, forming the words as I speak. "But I grew up on systems like the one you're trying to perfect. I didn't want to brag before, but I always won the hacking races we held. Always. And if anyone can find and fix flaws in that system of yours, it's me. You won't be disappointed, Mr. Fuller. I promise."

He studies me for a moment. If he's impressed, or annoyed, he doesn't show it. He merely stares at me with those icy blue eyes of his, drawing out a silence in the room, as if building up suspense.

"Call me Sully," he says absently. "Well, you've convinced me. When can you start?"

My jaw drops open again, and I force it closed.

Just like that, I'm in? Well, I guess he is the CEO, after all.

"Wow. I mean, uh, as soon as… tomorrow?" I stutter.

He chuckles good naturedly, his gruff facade cracking for a moment.

"There's no correct answer to that one, Marek. But if you can start tomorrow, that's excellent. I'll tell HR to get everything ready. Come in tomorrow, first thing. Friday's a great day for a first day, to show you the ropes and give you the weekend to get your head round everything."

He rises to his full height, towering over me. His broad and muscular physique, rather than intimidate, makes me feel strangely safe as I rise to my feet and look up at him.

"Eight-thirty," he continues. "We'll get you set up, and, well, then you can show us what you can do."

"Thank you, Sully," I say, and hold out my hand. His huge palm and fingers engulf mine as he takes it into a strong embrace, and I hold back a shudder of pleasure at his touch.

"Don't mention it. I've got a board meeting first thing. But I'll come check in on you when I can," he says gently. "Now go celebrate, play some games, have a drink or two, whatever."

Sully's final sentence is barked, almost like an order, and I nod seriously at him before making my way from the building, my feet feeling light underneath me, as if the whole experience had just been a daydream

That night I did exactly what Sully had asked, or rather ordered, me to do. I met my best friend Alice for a few glasses of wine and some dinner, and told her the good news. The wine helped me to unwind and relax somewhat, as my mind was still reeling.

I made my excuses to leave Alice in the early evening, despite various protests and her even bribing me with more wine. I knew I had to stay clear headed. OK, I know I'm a damn good codewriter and analyst, and accomplished hacker, but going in to my first day at work fuzzy headed is definitely a bad idea, especially with what's at stake.

So, I now find myself sitting in front of my pride and joy, in the office of my small outer-city apartment. A top-spec computer, with multiple screens and base units. I'm forever tinkering and adding to it, replacing outdated parts and building custom software to boost performance.

It's able to run high end games and design software with ease, alongside multiple complex decoding and artificial intelligence programs I have running in the background, without breaking a sweat.

But its performance isn't what I'm using it for right now.

Its anonymity.

I start up the custom VPN software I've created, rendering my computer all but invisible to even a well-trained eye, and open up a custom Dark Web browser.

Using a number of passwords and encrypted access codes, I log into the messaging group I use to communicate with my fellow ex-students. I need to let them know the good news, and that, so far, everything is going to plan.

I tap out a quick message and post it in an encrypted thread, as an extra layer of protection. Even then, only those who had access to the group would know what I was talking about.

FIRST STAGE OF MISSION; SUCCESS.
PROCEEDING WITH INFILTRATION AND
INVESTIGATION, BEFORE MOVING ON TO
FINAL STAGE. MONITOR THIS THREAD
FOR UPDATES.
CROW.

With the message posted, I shut down the programs one by one, and take a breath to steady my nerves. I'm both excited and scared, and I know I'll have to be at my best to achieve what I needed to.

An image of Sully flashes in my mind's eye, and I feel a pang of guilt, followed closely by a knot of butterflies in my stomach, which turns to a warm rush of sexual excitement.

Calm down Marek. Be professional. Though getting close to the CEO can't be a bad thing. And it might be damn-well enjoyable, too. Those big hands, that huge, muscular body...

I shudder as a wave of pleasure courses through my entire body, and then I shake the thoughts from my head as I start to prepare myself for the following day.

I arrive at the office ten minutes early, feeling a little nervous and out of place as I join the procession of serious looking, suit-clad men and imperious, smartly-dressed women all entering the high rise office of Fuller Securities Group.

The receptionist, the only other young person I've seen so far, greets me with a warm, genuine smile, and I feel a little more at ease as she signs me in with a temporary security pass.

"I hear Sully interviewed you all on his own," she says with a sly grin as she passes me the pass.

I smile at her briefly, and then search her sparkling eyes with a slight frown.

"Yeah. He's taking a very close interest in the project," I reply. "I think I'll be working fairly close with him. Well, for a while, at least. Until I get set up."

The receptionist leans forward.

"Lucky boy," she says in a low voice, with a wink.

I feel myself blushing slightly at her words, and thank her for her help before heading in to the building.

I study my reflection in the chrome metal of the lift door as I wait. I adjust my collar and snug sweater, smoothing out the wrinkles of my shirt, and adjusting the neckline of my V-neck sweater.

I am a late developer, and I'm still waiting on my beard to grow in one day. My narrow shoulders are clearly defined through the thin material of my tight sweater, and I might be a small guy but I'm not a weakling. I've got some swell to my biceps and I know how to flaunt them.

My narrow hips, lean thighs and slim waist are accentuated by my fitted, charcoal grey wool dress trousers, and I can feel my bubble butt pushed against the trousers by the perfectly tight fit my tailor was able to achieve in the back. Thank God that tailor knows what he's doing or else I'd look like I had the body of a puberty aged kid.

My hair hangs in natural curls, framing my face and hanging down just past my ears. Large, thick framed designer glasses obscure a little of my face, and I push them back up my nose, almost without thinking.

After a short lift ride to the middle floor of the huge building, I'm following the directions given to me by the receptionist, and before long I manage to locate the HR department, in order to begin my induction, and to get the multitude of non-disclosure agreements signed, so I can get started.

The induction takes most of the morning to complete, and my inductor takes me through a number of presentations, evacuation procedures, security protocols and privacy policies.

I try my best to pay attention, but the vast majority is just a boring, box ticking exercise, and I find my mind drifting on more than one occasion.

I'm excited about two things. Getting started with my work, and getting close personal attention from Sully.

He'd been gruff and surly when he'd interviewed me, for the most part. He seemed reserved and matter of fact, and I could tell straight away that he's ex-military, owing to the fact that my dad had served in the US Rangers, and carried the same air of calm, collected efficiency.

But at the same time, there'd been the almost imperceptible look that had flashed all so briefly in his eyes, as they met mine. And the brief cracks I'd seen in his facade, showing the man beneath, almost as if he's finally starting to shrug off his habitual military demeanor. I may be young, but I can tell when a man is checking me out.

All in all, I'm intrigued. And despite the seriousness of why I took the job in the first place, I figured letting Sully become a pleasant distraction wouldn't do any harm at all.

CHAPTER THREE

SULLY

The board meeting drags on, as it usually does, with one or two of the usual suspects enjoying the sound of their own voice a little too much, basking in the perceived glory of their elevated management positions.

I look around at the faces seated at the large, ornate wooden table. The ex-military are easy to spot. Immaculate suits, crisp, freshly ironed shirts. Bad haircuts. Sat upright, expressions guarded and stern, most glaring at the middle-aged, overweight director who looks like he wouldn't know which end of a gun to point away from himself.

He's carrying on with a dull, droning monologue about the perceived overzealousness of our security team, and the constant searches and security checks he has to endure.

I smile inwardly. Most of us who bothered to interact with the lower level employees, as I did, knew that he was targeted for regular security checks mainly because he was such an asshole, and the security teams had a sweepstake going for the most searches on him that they could get away with, with the winning team pocketing a cool few hundred dollars each at the end of the year.

OK, it was a little childish. But they had to stave off the boredom somehow, and it wasn't as if the guy didn't deserve it. He *is* an asshole, after all. Damn good at his job, but an asshole nevertheless.

I hold up my hand to interrupt him, feeling irritation rise as my precious time ticks by.

"Geoff, I think we've got it," I say sternly. "But these procedures are there for a reason. Hell, I had my office scanned for bugs, and my files audited on Tuesday, which wasted half my day."

I glance at the large blue face of my expensive silver watch. The meeting is running over time, as usual, and I have my mind on other things.

Like seeing Marek again.

"Look, I'll have a word with the guys personally. See if we can't reduce the regularity of these random spot checks, and ensure they are spread fairly."

I glance around the room, making eye contact with everyone as I speak, clapping my hands together and smiling.

"Now, as you all know, after months of hard work and each and every one of us sat at this table breaking our balls, we've finally got the go ahead from Mosner Corp to get Project Cutthroat pushed through into testing."

A ripple of surprise spreads in the room, with a few cheers from the more outspoken of the directors.

I stand to my feet, and spread my arms wide.

"So, if that's not a cause for celebration, I don't know what is!" I say in my booming, drill-ground voice. "All non-vital staff are to be given permission to leave a few hours early, and each team given an expense account for drinks and food, which I'll sign off personally."

I glance at the Director of Operations.

"Frank, if you could spread the good news?" I say, and he nods back with a grin.

"I'll be in O'Rourke's, three pm. Drinks are on me," I say as I make to leave the room. "The real work starts Monday."

I stride from the boardroom, smiling to myself as I make my way to the elevator. It was going to be an expensive day, with my sudden and unexpected gesture of generosity. But I can afford it.

Fifty thousand times over.

I sigh at the thought of my amassed wealth, and the diverse shares and investment portfolio I've created after deciding to reduce my stake in Fuller Corp, gradually over the last few years. I now had fifty-one percent of the shares, and I'm biding my time to sell a chunk of the remainder, and finally hand over the mantle of CEO to a capable deputy.

I brush aside my aspirations as I approach the secure section of our huge IT department, and swipe my security card to gain entry.

The heavy, reinforced glass door swings open with a pneumatic whoosh, and I glance around at the figures hunched, staring intently at computer monitors.

"Hey, did you see the email?" A hushed voice says excitedly as I pass. "We get off early today. Drinks on the company."

His colleague chuckles in response.

"Yeah. Maybe we could ask that new guy if he wants to join…"

Oh no, he won't be joining you. Because he'll be coming with me.

The voices fade as I head to where I'm guessing Marek is, at the center of the secure section. The hub of the Project Cutthroat, where our best and brightest security systems experts work.

My spirits lift as I see Marek, deep in conversation with the project lead, and intense look of concentration on his incredibly fine features. I'm frozen in place for a moment as I study him, my eyes lingering on his tight, lean figure as sexual desire courses through me, unbound.

He notices my attention, and glances up at me with a warm smile. My heart skips a beat, and I nod back and walk over to the pair.

The conversation stops, and the Project Lead looks up at me through thick glasses.

"Oh, hey boss!" he says excitedly. "I was just explaining to the young man where we're at so far with Project C. All the boring stuff, you know."

"Thanks, Carlos," I respond.

I grab a chair and join them, glancing from Carlos, back to Marek.

"So, we ready for a trail run of this baby yet or what? See what it's made of?" I say in a low, conspiratorial tone.

Marek's eyes widen with excitement, and he looks up at Carlos with a look of expectation.

"He's been inducted, signed all the ND docs. We aren't starting the rigorous testing until Monday, buuuut," his words tumble out, almost tripping over himself as his highly intelligent brain works at super speed. "I figure it wouldn't hurt to have a trial run. Test out the newbie."

Carlos grins at me.

"Sort of like an initiation. Trial by fire," he adds.

I look at Marek, to see a confident smile on his face.

"All right. Let's unleash our new hacking expert," I say. "I'll leave you guys to it."

I rise to my feet, towering over the pair for a moment.

"Marek, you've got until two-thirty. Report to me direct with your initial findings. My office is on the top floor," I add, before turning on a heel to leave.

The rest of the day is uneventful, to say the least. After reluctantly leaving Marek to his work, I grab a quick lunch and retire to the solitary sanctuary of my large, plush office. I can't help but feel excited that the project is finally up and running after the intense bidding process, followed by months of initial development.

I try to tell myself that the pressure isn't off yet, and that things are only just getting started, but the hard part, for me at least, has been done. Still, I'm determined to keep a close personal eye on how things progress, especially now Marek is on board.

There's something about him that intrigues me, a gut feeling that I can't quite place. Despite his sometimes quiet exterior, there's a confident core underneath, an almost visible strength of character he shows in brief flashes.

The afternoon passes slowly and without much interruption, and I use the time to plough through the pile of emails I've been neglecting for most of the week.

I lose track of time after a while, and I'm brought back to reality by the chirping of my desk phone. It's from my PA, and I pick up the receiver.

"Marek Williams here to see you, Sully?" she asks.

I glance at my watch. It's only two PM. I raise my eyebrows in surprise.

"Sure. Send him in," I respond.

I sit back in my chair, and glance over at the sound of a gentle knock on the door. Marek quickly enters, smiling shyly at me as he looks around in awe at the room, clutching a single sheet of paper.

He approaches my desk, and I gesture for him to take a seat opposite me.

"That was quick," I say, impressed. "What you got for me, Marek?"

He shuffles on his chair a little, glancing down at the handwritten notes he's clutching in his lap.

"Carlos and I ran the new security system on a stand-alone server," he says. "I acted as an external hacker, with no security clearance or direct means of access."

His bright eyes meet mine, shining with intelligence and enthusiasm.

"I was able to compromise the system to some extent, and with my initial study I found two major flaws, and a small number of minor glitches in the code that could be exploited. OK, they wouldn't result in a minor data breach, but - "

"But they could compromise the system and our data servers," I say, and he nods in agreement.

"So, what you're saying is," I continue, "that it needs improvement. Let's say we put you on perfecting the code, alongside Carlos. What would you suggest?"

Marek leans forward a little, and I catch a hint of his masculine scent, a citrusy cologne mixed with freshly-washed hair. I try desperately to keep my eyes from his body, but find myself glancing at his Adam's apple and the divet on his throat on occasion as he talks.

If he notices my attentions, he doesn't say anything, and starts to describe what we could do to begin improving the newly developed security system.

CHAPTER FOUR

MAREK

Sully listens intently as I talk through my findings in detail, and explain, as best I can, what I would suggest we could work on as a start to enhancing the security of the system, and further ways to test it.

To my surprise he seems fairly knowledgeable on the aspects of the system, and I don't have to dumb down what I'm saying anywhere near as much as I expect. There's a few times when he stops me to ask that I explain something in further detail, but I only have to explain once, and then he's committed the information to memory, just like that.

He's obviously not overly technically-minded, but he clearly has a disciplined, tactical intelligence that was forged in the military, or perhaps before, and honed in the years since.

As we talk, and I glance away briefly, to meet his eyes again, I notice that, when he can, he's checking me out. I'm not sure at first, but after a few minutes I definitely see his eyes drifting from mine for brief, almost imperceptible moments.

I feel a thrill at his attention on me, and an awakening of my newfound sexual confidence, and instead of shying away from the attention, I do my best to encourage Sully with my body language.

I don't have a lot of first hand experience with men and this is the first time I've ever attracted the attention of a guy as hot as Sully.

I lean forward on occasion, absently brush my locks of hair back behind my ear. I pout, or bite my lip when thinking, and occasionally look away shyly from his intense eye contact. We're talking about work, but there's a palpable subtext going on, and I delight in manipulating the chemistry between us.

Then, after an intense discussion, my ideas are exhausted, and I feel a little sad that it's come to an end, and that I'll soon be back at my work station, deep in the bowels of the huge building.

"So," I say. "What should I work on for the rest of the afternoon? Should I type up a report of my findings?"

Sully shakes his head, and stares intently at his watch for a moment, deep in thought.

"No need for a report," he replies, tapping his temple. "Got all your info safely stored in here. Plus, it was a test run. We'll sit down with Carlos on Monday, and get a plan of attack prepared for the real work."

I smile back, already looking forward to spending more time with Sully.

"In the meantime, that's us done for the day. Go and grab your stuff, and meet me down at main reception in five."

I slowly rise to my feet, frowning in confusion.

"What's… where are we going?" I ask.

He grins up at me from his plush leather armchair, his serious exterior fading away as he visibly starts to relax.

"Why, for a drink or three. Luckily for you, I've ordered a companywide event to celebrate the new contract, on your first day, no less."

His expression changes, and he looks momentarily guarded.

"I mean, that's if you'd like to join us, of course?" he adds.

I take a moment to respond, leaving him in suspense. But I already know my answer.

"Sure. That sounds good, Sully. See you downstairs?" I reply.

I wave at him as I turn to leave, feeling his eyes on me as I walk from the room.

Sully introduces me to his fellow directors and senior management that have joined us at the huge, impressive bar, and I feel a little out of place as he mentions each guy's job role.

There's a group of them standing at the bar, some with champagne, others with thick crystal tumblers containing large measures of whiskey. After brief introductions, Sully ushers me from the group, and I follow him to the bar.

"Sorry about that. They're good guys, but they don't really know how to have fun," he says apologetically. "They'll be talking about work. Some of 'em just don't know how to switch off."

He sighs, leaning on the bar with his elbows.

"Feels like something I've almost forgotten to do, sometimes," he adds quietly.

I feel a pang of compassion at his words. I can't even begin to comprehend the pressures he must experience at his level, and the effect it would have on someone's personal life.

Well, I can make him feel better, at least. I definitely haven't forgotten how to have fun. I sometimes even forget I'm not a student any more.

I wave over a bartender.

"Two cosmos please. And make 'em strong," I say.

Sully raises an eyebrow, mainly at my drinks choice, and likely because he was expecting to pay.

"What, so you too tough to enjoy a fruity cocktail every now and again?" I tease.

He shakes his head, and rises from his perched position to his full height. My eyes are at his chest level, and I have to crane my head to make eye contact, especially when we're standing so close.

"You're obviously a man who knows what he likes," he says, elbowing me playfully in the arm.

I smile at the gesture as our drinks are poured and brought over.

"To an exciting challenge," I toast, and we clink glasses.

I follow Sully over to a secluded booth, and I slide in opposite him as he takes a seat.

"So you want me all to yourself?" I ask coyly.

Sully shrugs.

"Well, I figure we should get to know each other a little better. We'll be working quite closely together for the next few weeks," he replies. "And, well... I guess you could say I enjoy your company."

His last few words are said almost as an apology, as if he expects me to want to be somewhere else.

But the reality is, there's nowhere else I'd rather be.

"I knew there was a person under that gruff exterior somewhere," I say, teasing. "So, if you don't mind me asking, where did you serve?"

He seems surprised at my question.

"How did you - "

I laugh good.

"My dad. He was a Ranger," I explain. "Well, he never really *stopped* being one, if you get what I mean. Just retired."

Sully chuckles at my words.

"I know exactly what you mean," he responds.

"Marines," he adds simply, pausing to take a sip. "I did a few tours of Afghanistan, then got relocated to Iraq."

He glances away for a moment, and touches a finger to a left shoulder without thinking, likely tracing the scar of an old war wound.

"I was a first lieutenant when my company got ambushed outside of Helmand. I was shot up pretty bad, but managed to get all my guys out of there in one piece before passing out in the Humvee on the way back to base."

A look of regret passes over him for a moment, as he pauses to drink again.

"I had aspirations, but it took me a long time to recover. So, I was honorably discharged, and so I turned my aspirations elsewhere," Sully adds, simply.

I feel an intense chemistry between us as he talks, and I know it probably isn't easy for him to talk about his career, cut short so early. I could see him as a stern-faced general, caring for his men more than he let on.

I place my hand on his forearm, bringing his attention back to me. He looks surprised at the gesture, but doesn't move to pull away.

"Well, things didn't turn out so bad in the end, right?" I say with encouragement. "Anyway, enough about work. What do you do for fun?"

We start to chat, mainly small talk. True to our word, we don't mention work, and the evening starts to pass, and we forget the world around as we drink and talk.

When Sully opens up, he's charming and funny, and even a little flirty. I make sure to flirt back, silently hinting that I like him on more than one occasion.

Evening turns to night, and we eat at our booth, not wanting to stop the flow of conversation between us.

After we've eaten, I take a sip from the glass of red wine I ordered with my meal, and glance around as a comfortable silence falls over us.

To my surprise, the bar is almost empty. We've been lost in our own little world for the entire evening, and all of Sully's fellow directors and cronies have long since left.

Sully follows my gaze, seeming to be just as surprised as I am at the deserted bar. He glances at his watch.

"This place is going to close soon," he says.

He opens his mouth to speak, but pauses. His eyes meet mine, and for a moment he doesn't seem to be able to find any words.

"Tonight's been great, Marek. I mean that. If it's not too much, how about we head back to my place for one or two more? My apartment's only a short walk from here," he says.

I raise my eyebrows.

Going back to his place on my first day at work? Wow. But I can't say no. The thought of getting him to myself, to see what that suit is hiding...

I smile up at him, and brush a stray curl of hair over an ear.

"Sure, I'd like that," I say, and we finish our drinks.

I rise to my feet, and Sully joins me, taking my arm in his.

"Lead the way, mister," I say, feeling a thrill of excitement at the prospect of breaking all of my usual rules.

Still, it's going to be worth it, I can tell.

CHAPTER FIVE

SULLY

Part of me is struggling to believe what's happening as I open the door to my penthouse apartment and guide Marek over the threshold with a gentle hand on his lower back. I still have a niggling gut feeling that I'm doing something wrong, but I put that down to the face that I can't even remember the last time I've brought a guy back to my place. Well, not since…

Don't think about it, Sully. It hurt, but that's in the past. You were young and naive, and thought you were invincible. A few high caliber rifle rounds changed all that, though.

I brush the sudden resurgence of long repressed memories aside, and focus on the present. On this young, hot guy stood in front of me, taking in his luxurious surroundings with something like awe on his delicate features.

"Wow," Marek says quietly. "Nice place you got here, Sully. It's huge!"

I grunt a laugh at his understated compliment.

"Yeah it isn't bad," I reply, walking past him to the kitchen. "It kind of loses its novelty after a while. Just feels like… a temporary home, you know?"

I feel a presence close to me, and glance over my shoulder to see Marek just behind me, watching as I prepare two glasses of expensive red wine.

"Temporary?" He asks softly.

The hairs on the back of my neck stand on end as his soft breath caresses my skin.

"Yeah. I've been thinking about stepping away from this lifestyle for a few years now. Find somewhere quiet to settle down. Find…" I hesitate for a moment, and turn to hand Marek a glass of wine. "A good man."

An unreadable emotion flashes behind his wide eyes, and he smiles shyly.

He leans on the counter of the bar behind him, glancing down momentarily. His boyish frame is well defined by the soft light directly above him. His face is illuminated, giving his pale skin an almost ethereal glow. He reminds me of Donatello's statue of David.

"Sully," he asks hesitantly. "I've been meaning to ask, and stop me if I'm crossing the line here."

I take a sip of wine, enjoying the deep flavors, and shrug, gesturing for him to continue.

"What do you make of this project? Of the company you have the contract with? I mean… well, why all this secrecy? Something doesn't sit right with me, is all."

His words strike a chord with me. I'd had the very same doubts myself, and had nearly avoided bidding on the contract. But the money had been too great. One last swan song to end my career on a high, I'd told myself at the time.

"I hear you," I respond. "But look, here's how things work. I… we only take on contracts based on a strict criteria. Obviously the money has to be right. Second, we don't deal with anyone on any blacklists. Companies selling to enemies of the state, rogue nations, terrorists, etc."

I choose my words carefully, conscious that I don't want Marek to distract himself with worries about morality.

"Finally, nothing that contravenes NATO conventions, and we try to avoid WMDs, unless we're dealing with the US government direct, of course. Other than that, we don't ask too many questions. If we did, well, we'd have gone bust a long time ago."

He looks up at me, a serious expression on his face as he digests my words.

"Look. I understand. But sometimes, in this game, you have got to just put those thoughts and doubts to one side, and focus on the job. If we hadn't taken the contract, someone else would. Don't lose any sleep over it, you hear?"

Marek nods decisively, seemingly placated by what I've said. Then he giggles, putting a hand over his mouth. His eyes widen in mock shock.

"Oh no! We said no work talk! Now I've done it," he says.

I shake my head and sigh.

"I'm disappointed, Marek," I say with a smile.

He places his glass down on the bar behind him, and slowly approaches. He stands in front of me, his body only a foot or so from mine.

"Let me make it up to you," he purrs.

I feel a surge of sexual desire course through me, and my mouth suddenly goes dry.

"Oh," I say. "And how exactly are you going to do that?"

He doesn't answer and simply takes a step forward, pressing his body against mine. I breathe in sharply at his proximity, and freeze for a moment.

Ok, Sully. Time to stop thinking...

I place my wine glass on the counter behind me, freeing both of my hands. Marek's body is still pressed hard against me, and he pushes his hips forward. I feel myself start to swell as the heat from his body seeps through my pants and I can feel his bulge.

He angles his face up towards me, and brings his lips slowly towards mine. Time seems to slow, and his eyes half close as he kisses me gently. I place my hands on his hips and pull him tight against me, kissing him back hard.

His tongue darts into my mouth, caressing mine, and he lets out a soft moan as we kiss. Then he pulls away suddenly, and brings his lips to my ear.

"I want you, Sully," he whispers, sending a thrill of pleasure down my spine.

His words are all the encouragement I need, and I finally know that he wants this to happen as much as I do. I find the hem of his sweater with my fingers, and slowly pull it upwards over his button up shirt.

Marek raises his arms and I pull the sweater over his head, throwing it to one side. He steps back from me and starts to unbutton his shirt, slowly revealing a large, Japanese style tattoo of a pair of koi fish that covers both sides of his entire chest. I'm a bit stunned; Marek didn't strike me as the huge tattoo type.

My breathing increases at the sight of his body as he slowly exposes the soft skin of his six pack abs and slim waist. I shake off my jacket in one swift movement, and it falls to the floor, forgotten.

My expensive, white silk shirt quickly follows suit as Marek reaches to my buttons, working them open one by one. His eyes widen as they rove my muscled and scarred torso. I barely notice as my own shirt slips from my shoulders, and he slowly slides it from my body.

His small nipples harden deliciously as they are exposed to the cool air in my apartment, and I'm eager to get them in my mouth. I marvel at the size of the koi tattoo, detailed and colorful, winding its way around his dark nipples visibly stiffened in the icy air of my air conditioned apartment.

"Wow," I say simply, taking a step forward.

Marek glances down at his own chest, then smiles up at me. His nipples brush against the skin of my stomach, and I feel a tingle of pleasure at the touch.

I place both of my hands on Marek's chest, tracing my fingers over the barely perceptible bumps and ridges of the tattoo. Despite the size of my huge hands and fingers, I can't cover the entirety of both fish with my grip. He lets out a soft moan as I tweak his hard nipples with my thumb and forefinger.

Marek deftly unfastens my belt as I slide my hands down to his toned waist. I feel myself hardening even more at the anticipation of pleasure, my erection almost painful within the confines of my tight underwear.

I reach a hand to unzip his trousers as he tugs at my pants to pull them down. I step out of them, and he gently slips his fingers under the hem of my boxer shorts, his eyes on mine as he slips them down my thighs.

My throbbing cock springs free from my underwear as he pulls them off, and I shudder as my tip brushes against the soft, warm skin of his lower belly. His eyes widen as he studies my length and girth with his mouth half open in surprise.

He slips out of his own trousers, his also hard cock jiggling visibly in his boxer briefs with the movement of his hips as he steps out of them once they hit the floor. Once free from his wool pants, he shimmies out of his own snug underwear, revealing a very handsome, delicious looking rock hard dick of his own.

His dick isn't as big as mine but its got a really nice curve to it, and I catch a glimpse of his neatly trimmed pubic hair in a small triangle just above the base, and I suddenly long to find out if Marek tastes as good as he looks.

Before I have a chance to reach down and stroke him, he's suddenly on his knees before me, bringing his face level with my incredibly hard cock.

CHAPTER SIX

MAREK

I drop to my knees in front of Sully, in awe of his muscular physique and his smooth, tanned skin. His heavily muscled chest and stomach are both adorned with a number of old battle wounds; I can see at least four bullet holes and a number of long, faded diagonal cuts.

The scars only serve to make him even more damn hot than he would be otherwise, and as I look up to meet his eyes, I trace my fingers delicately over a long scar on his rock hard abs, eliciting a shudder of pleasure across his skin.

He watches me, eager and wide eyed, his cheeks flushed with desire as I take his huge cock in my right hand, squeezing his shaft hard. My small hand doesn't even encompass his girth, and my fingers don't meet as I wrap them around him.

I use my left hand to accentuate the circular movement of my right as I start to jerk him off, and Sully groans loud and long at the sensation. I move my hands slowly but firmly, rocking back and forth on my legs to aid the movement of my hands and arms.

He pushes forwards with his hips, bringing his bulging glans inches from my face. I oblige, opening my mouth wide and holding his eye contact as I take him inside my lips. The smooth skin of his tip brushes against my tongue as his girth stretches my mouth wide, and my eyes widen as I take as much of him as I can.

Even with his cock almost to the back of my throat, and my two hands in front of one another, there's still a good few inches of his shaft left. Sully moans as I run my tongue in circles around his glans, using my lips to caress his shaft and sucking him as I rock back and forth.

He places his hands on the back of my head, guiding me gently, urging me to take as much of him as I can. He moans encouragingly, his legs shaking a little at the pleasure I'm giving him. I feel myself getting hot and harder between my legs, and I wonder if I can even take his huge manhood inside me as I kneel before him, giving myself over to him in submission.

His cock twitches in my mouth, and I slow my movements, not wanting him to finish early and deny myself the pleasure of having him inside me. I look up to see Sully's eyes closed, his head back and a frown of deep pleasure on his handsome face. He slowly opens his eyes as I stop sucking him.

He leans down to place a hand under either of my armpits, guiding me to my feet with incredible strength. Then, I'm suddenly in the air as he lifts me effortlessly from my feet, and walks forwards to place my butt on the surface of the bar behind me.

Sully steps back and grips my hip bones with both of his hands, and roughly pulls my body to the edge of the bar, so close that I might fall off if he wasn't holding me. His expression is that of near desperation as he seems overcome by an animalistic desire to take me.

I shudder in anticipation as he quickly pulls open a drawer and produces a small bottle of what I assume is lubricant, and then Sully places a strong hand under either of my thighs, pushing my legs wide and standing before me, his massive erection standing proud just inches from my own hard on.

His eyes devour every inch of my naked body, and I perch myself up on my elbows to accentuate the arch of my back. He watches as I twist a nipple with my right hand, biting my lips and letting out a soft moan of sexual desire.

I run my hand down over my body, reaching for my throbbing hard manhood, and grasp my shaft in my hand, stroking it gently, working out a drip of precum at the tip. Sully's eyes widen at the gesture, and I smile seductively at him.

"Come here and fuck me, Sully," I say in a strained, pleading voice. "I want to feel you inside me…"

He pushes my legs back and up, hard, and I gasp as he slowly thrust forwards with his hips. His cock presses against the opening of my ass for a moment. I shudder involuntarily in anticipation as I wait in agonizing torment, longing to be filled by his manhood.

Then he pushes himself into me, gasping as he steps forward on his feet to slide his impressive length slowly deeper and deeper into my body. The sensation is like nothing I've ever felt before as he fills me up, slowly and gently, and the walls of my ass stretch to their limit around his girth.

After a moment I feel his hips slap against my thighs and butt, and I know I've somehow managed to take all of him. My eyes half close at the almost painful pleasure I feel deep inside me, spreading from my ass to my stomach, and sending waves of pleasure through my entire body.

I moan with wordless encouragement, nodding and gasping, moaning for Sully to fuck me hard and fast. He keeps his movements slow and controlled, sliding his shaft back out of my slick hole, before pushing himself deep into me again.

As he fucks me, he starts to increase in speed, and his muscles bunch deliciously with both effort and pleasure. He lets out a low, animalistic groan, gritting his teeth and grunting in time with his thrusts.

I place one hand on my own cock, stroking away and my other hand on his hips and pull him towards me hard, encouraging him to let himself go, and take me until he climaxes. He somehow manages to keep control of himself, despite the shuddering pleasure of my hot, naked body.

I suddenly realize that I'm moaning his name in encouragement, and our eyes lock for a long moment. I feel something pass between us, some sort of understanding or connection, and it's almost as if he senses the orgasm coming on strong within me.

All of a sudden, Sully loses control, giving himself over to his base urges, and he thrusts into me hard, fast and deep, his hard muscles slapping against my soft skin. He grips my hips hard for purchase, pulling my body close to his with each thrust, filling me with his rock hard cock over and over.

"Oh, Sully," I manage to say between gasps. "Yeah that's it. Fuck me hard…"

My whole body convulses as I start to climax, and I feel my balls clench. The sensation is incredible, electric waves of pleasure shooting from my prostate, through my balls and up into my body. An explosion of pleasure, fueled by endorphins and the release of tension sweeps through my being.

"Marek," Sully says in desperation, a growl escaping as waves of pleasure rack his body.

I can barely think, let alone respond, and I simply nod encouragement up at him as our eyes meet. He lets out a soft shout of pleasure as he finally loses all control, his thrusts now deep and slow as he starts to orgasm.

His cock throbs inside me as he orgasms, and another wave of pleasure rolls over me as he shoots his hot cum deep into my core. He shudders and moans, all of his muscles clenching tight, his thrusts now slow and erratic.

With one final push, his cock drives deep into me, and I feel a deep glow of satisfaction spread through me as his orgasm fades, and he stands there before me, gasping for breath.

Sully leans forward on his hands for support as he recovers his energy momentarily. He smiles a satisfied smile at me, and I let out an approving moan of pleasure as our eyes meet.

We both stay silent for a long moment, simply enjoying the afterglow as we study each other, both equally in awe with what had just passed between us. I'd never felt a connection like this before, and I'm struck dumb momentarily.

"Well," I say, after a minute. "That sure was something."

He grunts in approval, standing back up and studying my naked body. He's recovered quickly, the realization of what we've just done together spreading over his features.

"Yeah. It sure was," he replies simply.

He smiles suddenly, and makes eye contact with me again.

"And," he continues, "it's still early. Did I tell you I have a Jacuzzi? And some champagne on ice?"

And here I was, thinking this night couldn't get much better.

But it sure did.

CHAPTER SEVEN

SULLY

F riday night's activities seem like a distant, almost surreal memory as I sit at my desk. It's Wednesday morning, and Project Cutthroat's rigorous testing phase is now in full swing.

I've spent as much time as possible with Marek, still in awe of my feelings for him, but wary that I need to let him focus on his job as much as possible. Still, I can't get him out of my mind, and I find him a pleasant distraction at all hours of the day.

We've decided to keep things secret for now, given the sensitive nature of the work we are doing together, and neither of us wanting to put too much pressure on whatever this turns out to be between us.

The first phase of testing has Carlos and his team, including Marek, following up on his initial findings from last week's brief study. Despite their expertise, after two days none of them have so far been able to identify all of the flaws he exposed in two hours.

I smile to myself at the thought. It almost seems like this was fate, both of us meeting over my final project as CEO of Fuller industries, with a whole world of opportunities ahead of me, and possibly us, when everything came to fruition.

I stop my train of thought, and bring my focus back to reality through the haze of my long daydream.

Don't get ahead of yourself, Sully. Remember what jumping in with two feet did last time.

Despite my own warning, I can't help but feel a deep connection to Marek. Plus, I'm used to getting what I want. And I want *him*.

I sigh wistfully and rise to my feet. Carlos is soon due to give a mid-week presentation to update the senior members of the project team, who aren't directly involved in the active development of Project Cutthroat, but have a vested interest in those working on it, or the outcome.

I leave my office to head to the meeting room, eager to see how things were progressing, and to lay my eyes on Marek once again.

"In summary," Carlos says, turning away from the projector screen to address the small audience. "We're on track, as things stand. OK, we all know the deadline for preliminary testing is right, but I think we're on track to get a beta build up and running in time."

He smiles and glances to my right. I follow his gaze, my eyes settling on the handsome face of Marek, who's sat next to me.

"I must admit, the new specialist addition to our team is, well... putting us all to shame."

An amused murmur spreads throughout the room. Marek blushes a little at the praise, and his eyes flick to meet mine momentarily.

I feel something brush against my thigh under the table, and reach down to find Marek's hand caressing me through the thin material of my suit pants.

I grasp his hand in mine and give him a squeeze, pressing his warm hand against my thigh in encouragement.

"He managed to expose more flaws in the system in his first quick once over than the whole team has found so far this week, following up on his findings," Carlos continues. "So, after a little discussion with the guys and gals, we've come up with an idea to streamline our work process."

Marek's hand is now on my inner thigh, running from my knee up towards my crotch. I feel a twinge of sexual tension building in my stomach, and my heart rate increases as he caresses me.

I hold back a shudder as he starts to stroke my cock through my pants, feeling myself start to swell at his gentle teasing.

"What do you propose then, Carlos?" I ask, needing all of my discipline to keep my voice steady.

He glances at the senior management and executives around the table in turn.

"With your permission, I'd like Marek to lead on the front end testing. I'll supervise and review, of course, but this will free up the rest of the team to implement changes based on his findings."

I nod in approval, keeping a straight face as Marek grabs my shaft and starts to jerk me off slowly.

"OK, I know it's, what? His fourth day? But I think Sully will agree he's more than shown us how capable he is," Carlos adds.

Oh, I agree. He's more than capable.

Marek grips me hard, and my erection swells painfully within the confines of my tight boxer shorts.

"I'm inclined to agree with Carlos," I say.

I grab Marek's hand under the table, rubbing him up and down the length of my stiff shaft.

"As long as the rest agree, I don't see why this won't work," I continue. "Guys?"

The plan is voted in without objection, and the meeting comes to a close. I pick up my briefcase before standing, using it to tactically cover my arousal as I rise to my feet.

"One thing Carlos," I say. "I'd like to talk this through further with Marek in my office, before we get things rolling. Just to make sure we're... going at it from the right angle, and that he knows we're all behind him on this."

Marek smiles at my innuendo, glances eagerly from me to Carlos, then back to me.

"Sure thing, boss," he replies. "Keep him for as long as you want, it's too late in the day to start something new. We'll get started with the new process first thing."

I follow Marek from the room, my eyes on his bubble butt and the soft curls of his hair. I step forward to join him at his side, and we walk down the corridor towards the elevators.

"Please tell me we aren't going to your office to talk about work?" Marek whispers, his voice dripping with desire.

I glance down at him with a sly smile as we wait side by side for the elevator. He pouts up at me, his full lips pursed suggestively.

"I just think it would be good for us to thrash things out, just you and I, until we're entirely satisfied. Don't you?" I say quietly.

We manage to make our way through into my office without any of my secretarial staff noticing. I close the heavy wooden door behind us, lock it, and close the blinds.

I walk over to my desk and pick up the receiver of my phone, and ring through to my PA.

"Yes. Hold all my calls. Mister Williams and I have a conference call with the client to discuss progress on Project Cutthroat momentarily. Hold my calls for the next hour," I lie.

I wink at Marek. He slowly starts to unbutton his dress shirt as I watch, distracted from what my PA is saying.

"Yes, that's fine. I'll deal with any messages first thing. Thank you. Oh, and why don't you take the rest of the afternoon off? Yes, I'm sure. Go enjoy the sunshine."

I place the receiver down and mute my phone, allowing my attention to be solely focused on the delicious young man slowly stripping naked in the middle of my office.

"So, Mr. Fuller, sir. Where do you want me?" Marek asks in mock professional tone.

He's wriggling out of his grey slacks, the bulging flesh of his cock already prominent within the confines of his boxer briefs.

I sweep the cluttered papers and folders, and a few desk ornaments, from the surface of my big wooden desk down onto the floor, and point at it.

"Come here and sit," I order in an authoritative voice.

Marek approaches the desk slowly, holding eye contact as he places his hands on the ornate wooden surface.

I unfasten the belt of my suit pants, and drop them to the floor. I pull my boxers down too, relieved to free my hard cock, and it stands proud and erect in front of me.

He sits on the desk, facing towards me, his legs dangling over the side, his cock struggling against the confines of his black underwear.

"Like this?" he asks me softly, his voice thick.

I nod, and his eyes widen as I sit down in my armchair in front of him.

"Take your underwear off," I command.

Marek obliges, quickly stripping off and stepping out of his underwear and throwing it to one side of the office. His erection bounces at the movement, swaying wonderfully from side to side.

He settles down on his elbows and watches me as I pull my chair up until I'm seated right in front of his body. His cock is swollen and pink, his arousal plain to see. He parts his legs obligingly, watching as I study the curve of his member. I can see his stomach clench and his balls tighten as my breath grazes his delicate skin.

I lean slowly forward to bring my mouth towards his sex, stopping to kiss his inner thighs momentarily. His legs shake and he gasps with frustration as I tease him, kissing round everywhere but his dick for a long moment, building up the anticipation of my mouth on him.

"Taste me," he urges, stroking my hair with a hand. "I'm yours. Do what you want to me."

I look up and hold his gaze as I lean further forward, taking his cock deep into my throat.

CHAPTER EIGHT

MAREK

Pleasure shoots through me as Sully buries my cock inside his throat, his mouth and tongue flicking at my glans. He sucks at me for a moment, and I gasp loud at the sensation as he pleasures me.

I grab his hair with both hands and push his head hard into me, amazed at how good his tongue feels as Sully runs his tongue in slow circles around my head. I let out a loud moan, uncaring if the office isn't sound-proofed. If we have an audience, well, they'd only be listening if they're jealous.

And they aren't getting what I am, right now. Sully, all to myself, his face nuzzling at my sex, his saliva spreading all over his handsome features.

I gasp as he soaks two big fingers with spit and pushes one inside me. Despite the size, I'm so horny that it slides into my ass with ease. I watch Sully as he devours my cock, licking and sucking on me as his finger searches for my prostate.

He grabs his huge cock with his free hand and starts to slowly jerk himself off as he pleasures me, and the sight of him playing with himself sends a shiver of sexual pleasure down my spine, accentuating the feeling of his mouth and tongue on me.

I let out another loud moan of satisfaction as my head starts to throb and tingle with every movement of his tongue.

"Sully, I want you to fuck me," I moan. "I need you inside of me."

He groans into my crotch at my words, his hand speeding up as he works his shaft, his legs opening wide and his hips thrusting forward. My whole body shudders and my asshole starts to spasm as I begin to climax.

Then, suddenly, he sits back on his armchair, his finger sliding from my ass, still glistening with his saliva. His face is flushed and wet from the sloppy blow job, and there's an eager look in his eyes as he studies me.

I stay where I am for a moment, letting him study my naked body for a moment while I watch him jerk himself off slowly. He places his free hand under my knee and pulls me forward, and I slide from the desk, standing flat on my feet before him.

The arms of the chair won't let me wrap my legs around him. I turn so I'm facing away, and slowly lower myself into his lap. Sully grabs my butt with a hand, and guides his cock into me as I settle down onto him.

I'd almost forgotten the incredible sensation of feeling him inside me as I push myself slowly downward, his shaft sliding into my slick asshole, stretching me wide. I hear Sully grunt behind me as he enters me.

He takes his hand from my butt and I drop suddenly into his lap, and his entire length is inside me within a second. I let out a soft scream of almost painful pleasure, gritting my teeth in awe at his incredible size.

"Ride me, Marek," he urges in a thick voice. "Ride me until you come."

His hands are all over my body as I start to ride him, sliding up and down his solid shaft, my tight ass enveloping his glans and shaft. I can feel him throb and shudder with every movement, adding to the pangs of pleasure I can feel deep within me.

I want nothing more than to feel his cock pulse as he comes inside me, but I control myself, gently easing him towards climax, knowing the longer I wait the better it will feel when I orgasm myself.

Sully grabs my dick in his large hand and strokes it hard, using his grip to guide me harder and faster. I place my hand on his, caressing his skin as he plays with my sensitive member, guiding his fingers to move harder and faster.

"Oh, god," he moans in my ear.

I look back over my shoulder and make eye contact with him. He grunts every take I take him inside me, gritting his teeth in an attempt to control himself.

"Sully," I gasp. "You're so big. My body feels so full right now."

He inhales sharply at my words, and I feel his cock twitch inside me, his strong and hard muscles clenching powerfully. I gasp at the sensation, and ripples of pleasure flow into my core.

I'm riding him hard and fast now, my butt slapping against his thighs with each thrust. I turn back to kiss him, our tongues writhing against one another. Sully's masculine scent of aftershave and fresh sweat rolls over me, and I even taste him in my mouth.

I run my hands over the taut muscles of his chest and stomach, marveling at how strong and solid he is. I'm enjoying being in control and pleasuring him, but part of me wants him to take me, to fuck me hard and fast until he comes.

It's almost as if Sully has read my thoughts as he rises suddenly to his feet, driving his cock deep into me. I gasp in surprise and pleasure as he bends me over his desk, and I press my body onto the wooden surface for support as he starts to thrust into me, again and again.

He grabs my hair, pulling my head back, and I moan his name loud. His thighs slap against my butt, and his balls hit my own hard, adding to the intense pleasure I can feel inside me.

The desk shakes with each of Sully's powerful thrusts. Some objects fell into the carpeted floor, but I barely even notice. The only thing that matters is what I'm feeling right now, this big and powerful man fucking me from behind, his moans loud and animalistic.

He grabs my hips and pulls my body back towards him. I feel a powerful sensation building deep within me, and I suddenly realize that I'm about to climax.

"That's it baby. Fuck me hard," I moan. "I'm coming, Sully. Yes!"

My voice is trained with pleasure, and I shudder violently as I orgasm. Sully slows his thrusts, but pushes as hard as he can into me as I ride the waves of pleasure shooting through my body.

I let out a yelp with every rhythmic spurt of my cum, and my dick feels like it's exploding with an intense, searing sensation that's as close to pain as it is pleasure.

Sully's completely in control, and I bend before him, supine and trembling.

"Oh, fuck…" he says loudly.

With that, he shoots his load deep into me, grunting and thrusting erratically as the orgasm sweeps over him. I look back over my shoulder at Sully, to see him grimacing as he comes, and his hands grip my hips hard.

His orgasm lasts for a long time, and I can feel his body trembling as he slows down his thrusts. I maintain eye contact with him as he finishes, and then collapse onto the desk, both of us breathless and spent.

He pulls out of me and places his hands either side of my body. I feel his lips on my neck, and his teeth nibble at my skin as he kisses me tenderly.

"I think that's the best thing that's ever happened in my office," he says after a moment.

I laugh at his words, and turn over so I'm looking up at him.

"And you know what the good thing is?" I ask him.

Sully shakes his head before standing back upright, his cock still hard and soaked with saliva and cum, and my skin tingles as it brushes my legs.

"That's just the first time we've done it in here."

He glances over to a door over to one side of the room.

"Good thing I've got an en-suite shower. Let's go get cleaned up," he says.

He picks me up onto my feet and places his arms around me as we walk to the bathroom, his warm body pressed hard against mine. I wonder how it's going to be possible to get any work done at all, now I know what we could get up to in his office.

CHAPTER NINE

SULLY

I t's been a week since Marek was given the privileged role of identifying flaws in the system, one which he's taking incredibly seriously, according to all accounts. From what I've heard from him, and the rest of the team, he's almost at a point where the majority of the major issues should have been identified.

Once that task is complete, he'll be back working with the team, fixing the system over an intense final few days before the initial deadline, in order to present the beta build to Mosner Corp's board and tech specialists for an initial review.

"We *have* to get this right," I say, addressing Carlos and his team.

We're in Project Cutthroat's final beta phase review meeting; an end of the day get together to make sure the team is ready for the frantic couple of days ahead of us.

I look at each of the tech specialists in turn, holding eye contact for a long moment, my expression set and serious. Some look away from my intense gaze, others nod back.

Marek winks at me, and I resist the urge to smile back.

"The guys at Mosner can still pull this from Fuller Industries. As you all know, they're entitled to by contract, up until approval of the alpha build," I continue.

I pace back and forth at the front of the room. All eyes are on me, and I'm enjoying the rapt attention to my almost military style speech.

"So. I want everyone to be clear on what they need to do, and be willing to break their real," I glance briefly at the two women in the room. "Or proverbial, balls. You got that?"

A murmur of approval ripples through the listening group.

"Good. All necessary overtime has been pre-approved by me, personally. Like I said, I don't want to go begging to Mosner for an extension. These guys don't fuck about. They'll laugh at me, and tell me where to shove it."

I stop my pacing and lay my hands flat on the large meeting room table.

"We've been over everything, but if you got a problem or question, now's the time. Carlos is going to be like your fairy godmother for the next few days. You got a problem? Tell him. You fucked up? Tell him. You're secretly in love with him and it's distracting you from your work? Tell him."

Carlos almost spits out a mouthful of coffee in a fit of laughter.

"I'll help out where I can, but computers and I just don't get on. Give me a hundred well-trained and heavily-armed soldiers and I could topple a rogue nation, but I don't think that's really an applicable skill here."

I pause and stand back up.

"Questions?" I ask the room.

Silence.

"Good. Get your shit ready and we'll hit this hard first thing. Doughnuts and coffee are on me. Hell, I'll even bring them to you," I add. "Carlos?"

He looks up at me.

"Yes boss?" he replies.

"I want you to review Marek's progress report, check he's good to move on to help out the rest of the guys with getting the code up to scratch. We need all hands on deck from here on out. Come see me before shift tomorrow, my office, at eight a.m. We'll have a last minute brief."

He nods seriously.

"Got it," he says.

I clap my hands together and bunch my jaw for a moment.

"All right. We're done here. Let's do this!" I say, my voice rising to a shout.

A couple of guys cheer approvingly as everyone rises to their feet to leave. Marek smiles at me and waves just his fingers, the last to leave the meeting room.

Here we go. All or nothing. Just how I like it.

"Y ou have got to be fuckin' shitting me," I say, overcome with shock. "I'm dreaming right now. I'll wake up in a minute, and start this day all over again. You'll come through that door, and tell me everything's A-fucking OK."

Carlos shakes his head, looking at his feet as he sits slumped in the chair opposite my desk. Anger wells up inside me at his words, and I get a sudden bitter taste in my mouth as I shake my head in disbelief.

"I wish it weren't true, Sully. You know that. But I spent the whole night checking, double checking. I barely slept. Had to sleep on the couch in case my wife cut my balls off for waking the baby up," he replies. He smiles weakly, a smile that fades as soon as it has come.

I take a long breath in through my nose, and exhale slowly, focusing my mind on what needs to be done.

"Right, listen and listen close. This isn't the end yet, you hear?" I say decisively.

Carlos perks up at my words, straightening his back and fixing me with an intense stare.

"Everything goes ahead as planned. What you've just told me doesn't leave these four walls. I want to see the normal Carlos leave this room," I continue. "Let's hope this is some sort of monumental oversight, or just a plain mistake."

I grunt at my own words.

"But we both know that isn't true. Anyway. There's only one person who can tell us the truth, and get us out of this mess," I say.

"Marek," Carlos replies grimly.

"Marek," I reply. "Send him direct to my office as soon as he gets through that door. Don't say a word. I need to see the look on his face when he hears what I have to say. If he comes clean, tells us how to fix this, maybe, just maybe, he gets a second chance."

It's Carlos' turn to grunt sardonically.

"Or this whole project is FUBAR," he says in a matter of fact tone.

I wave a dismissive hand.

"That's for me to worry about. You got any shares in Fuller?" I ask.

He shakes his head, grinning.

"Well then," I add. "Isn't a big deal. Go get this show on the road. We aren't going down without a fight."

He springs to his feet, his usual enthusiasm visibly returning. He nods and turns on his heel to get his team ready for a hectic day.

When he's gone, I slump in my chair, overcome by a feeling of betrayal that makes me feel sick. My mind wanders, and time becomes meaningless as I go over and over the past few weeks in my head, trying to make sense of everything.

Did he even like me in the first place? Or was I being used all along? But what I felt was so real, tangible even. There's got to be something else going on here, I can feel it. It can't end like this.

An indeterminable amount of time later, the door of my office swings open, and a confused Marek enters. He smiles at me for a second, but the smile soon fades when he sees the grim expression on my face.

"Hey, Sully. You asked to see me?" Marek says quietly.

He approaches the chair opposite, his expression a little anxious and guarded. His cheeks are flushed a soft pink, and his eyes are wide with what seems like the onset of panic.

"Sit," I growl.

He obliges, taking a seat opposite my imposing desk. I sit looking at him for a moment, trying my best to shake off my feelings for him. Which proves more difficult than I had imagined it would.

"I spoke to Carlos earlier. He told me about your work," I say with quiet menace. "Exposing flaws and manipulating the code to hide them, and not reporting the whole thing to Carlos, or to me? Do you think we're all idiots, Marek?"

Marek visibly flinches at my words, and his handsome face flushes a deep shade of crimson.

"Sully, please! I - "

"Do *not* bullshit me Marek," I say quickly, interrupting him. "You are this close to a very serious confidentiality breach with me, and with Mosner."

He glances away, looking ashamed.

"And trust me," I continue, "that is really not a place you want to be."

I take a deep breath to calm myself again, not wanting my anger and emotions to cloud my judgment of this screwed up situation.

"Was this whole thing between us just a ploy? So you could earn my trust and then use me?" I ask.

He shakes his head, and a single tear rolls down a flushed cheek. I feel an unfamiliar pang of emotion in my chest, something I haven't felt for over a decade as I study him.

Damn you, boy. If you're still playing me, then I have no hope. You better just come clean and see if I have the heart to forgive you.

I clear my throat to attract Marek's attention. He looks up at me, eyes wide and head lowered, waiting for me to speak.

"For what happened between us, I'm going to give you one chance. *One* chance, Marek, to explain to me what the fuck is going on. Now."

Marek sits up a little straighter in his seat, and a look of quiet determination appears in his eyes as he studies my features for a moment.

"OK," he says in a serious tone. "I'll explain. But you got to listen to me until I'm finished, OK?"

I nod, and he takes a moment to collect his thoughts before telling me everything.

CHAPTER TEN

MAREK

My heart is pounding in my chest, and I swear I can hear its beat rushing in my ears as Sully glares at me. His features are set and composed, but his eyes are burning with anger and betrayal.

My gut twists at being caught out, and the situation I'm now in. But I knew the risks. Getting romantically involved with Sully was always going to be a gamble, but my feelings for him are genuine, and my betrayal breaks my heart.

Still, he's giving you a chance. Now's the time, Marek. If you truly care for him, let him in. You know he'll be on your side, as long as he understands everything.

"I'm a hacker, Sully," I say after a moment.

His glare intensifies.

"I know that. Care to give me something I don't know?" he replies.

I shake my head.

"No. I mean, I'm a hacker. Hacktivist, vigilante, spy. Whatever you want to call it."

He raises an eyebrow a little. From what I can tell, this isn't a surprise to him.

"I knew about Mosner Corp before I even saw the job listing," I continue. "I have been looking for a way to expose them to the public for a long time now.

"Look. I have a gift, Sully. Code to me is like words. I can read it, instantly see what even the most trained hacker or coding specialist would take weeks to figure out. And a long time ago, I asked myself - how will I use this gift?

Sully leans forward on his elbows, his blue eyes boring into my soul as he stares at me intensely, waiting for me to carry on.

"Do you actually know what Project Cutthroat is?" I ask.

Sully frowns at me.

"Of course I do. Next-gen weapon systems for the US and a few select allies," he responds.

I shake my head.

"That's the official line," I say sadly. "But let me guess - the exact details of what they're developing aren't really detailed anywhere. Not even you - with the highest level security clearance on the project team - has a clue what you're helping to hide."

I pause for a moment to take a breath, adding to the dramatic effect of my impromptu speech.

"Biological warfare."

He flinches at my words, an incredulous expression on his strong features.

"What? But... I thought we left that shit behind in the eighties?" he says, almost choking.

"Not just any biological warfare," I add. "A sophisticated, engineered virus that is being designed to become more effective than a nuclear weapon when targeted at a population center."

Sully's face whitens, and his eyes fix on a space in the middle distance for a moment.

"I can't... how do you know all of this? How do I know you aren't bullshitting me, Marek?" he says quietly.

His eyes flick back to focus on mine, and I stare at him, imploring him to believe me. I know my next few words will make or break this whole thing.

"Sully, I didn't mean for us to… you weren't part of my plan," I say, feeling another tear roll down my cheek. "I could have done this without using you, and I hope you understand that. What's happened between us is real. I've fallen for you, and whatever you decide, whatever happens now, my feelings for you will never change."

I pause for a moment to collect my thoughts before continuing.

"I've got a contact on the inside. A mole. A guy I used to be friends with in college. If you think what I've done is difficult or underhand, try infiltrating Mosner Corp from the inside, without getting caught. Their systems are so robust, constantly monitored by the world's best security techs, it's a wonder he hasn't been found at, and made to… 'disappear.'"

Sully grunts at my words.

"Which is something they have been accused of doing in the past," he says slowly.

I nod at him.

"Exactly. Anyway, he's got as far as he can, and now he's shit scared. He can't suddenly quit his job for fear of any suspicion. So, he is *literally* going to disappear to the other side of the world, as soon as I give him the green light. That's how serious this is, Sully."

He rolls his shoulders back and then frowns suddenly.

"What about you? Were you just going to… disappear, too? Without a word?" he asks.

"No. Well, I hadn't really got that far. This really hasn't worked out the way I planned it to, believe me," I admit. "But now, I don't want to leave. I don't want to be anywhere where you're not."

I hope the sincerity of my words comes across as much as I meant it. To my relief, Sully's expression softens momentarily.

"So, this biological warfare you mentioned Mosner are planning on developing. How bad is it, exactly?" he asks.

I sit up a little straighter as I start to see a dim light at the end of this dark tunnel I've created.

"A virus. And virulent doesn't even begin to describe how bad it could be. The idea is to develop a deadly, highly contagious and fast acting virus that shuts down the central nervous system and kills over ninety-nine percent of victims within three to four minutes.

"Even those with powerful immune systems will stand no chance - a cytokine storm, caused by their own overactive immunities, would do just as much damage as the virus itself."

I sigh at the unimaginable horror that the virus would wreak if ever unleashed, yet feel a strengthening of my resolve as I come clean to Sully.

"If the virus was released in a population center, it would kill so fast that it would burn out quicker than it could spread past the limit of the city. Imagine - if you're dead in three minutes, how far would you get? Planes wouldn't leave the runway. People would only get a few blocks away from their house before... well, you get the picture.

"Hence why it would be a more controlled and destructive weapon than a nuke. And relatively little damage to infrastructure in comparison. A whole country could be neutralized in a matter of hours."

I pause to take a breath, and for dramatic effect. Sully's handsome face is twisted with concern, and possibly anger. I know he's finding it hard to believe what I'm saying.

But I can prove it.

"The perfect weapon," he whispers in awe.

I frown at Sully.

What did he just say?

"Take out your enemy without losing a single man. Then move in to occupy without resistance. But... all that collateral. All those innocent lives..." he continues, almost as if talking to himself.

He fixes me with an intense glare.

"And what if they were to miscalculate? What if a small number of people had a previously unknown genetic immunity to this virus, and it spread across the globe? We'd be talking the end of, well, everything," he continues. "No. No, this isn't right."

He stands suddenly, his shoulders set, muscles bunching beneath his well-fitted suit. He runs his hands through his thick hair, staring out of the window momentarily for inspiration.

To me, he looks like a hero. Strong, yet kind and gentle, confident and immovable. If I have him on my side, then there's no stopping us.

"I believe you, Marek," he says finally. "It all makes sense now. I knew as soon as you walked into the interview room that something didn't sit right with this whole damned thing. But I need you to show me. I need to see it with my own eyes. Can you do that?"

I'm startled at how quickly he's made his mind up.

"Of course, Sully. I can get the info from my contact. It's nothing solid enough to go to the press with - hence my involvement here - but it's enough to show you how serious this is," I reply.

He starts to pace in front of me, his left hand supporting his right shoulder; his right hand rubbing at his strong jaw.

"You're fired" he says suddenly.

I choke at his words.

"What?"

He smiles at me.

"You're fired, Marek. For a breach of confidentiality. When you leave this room, go straight for the stairs and head back to your station."

Sully is speaking quickly, formulating a plan even as the words tumble from his mouth.

"I'll call Carlos up here. He'll take the lift, obviously, so you won't pass each other. I can get you ten, maybe fifteen minutes before you'll have to leave the building. I can't risk anything more than this, or questions are going to start getting asked. Carlos knows what you've been doing. Hell, I reckon he already knows everything."

"So, you go back. Don't talk to anyone, act as if nothing has happened. Fifteen minutes, Marek, to implement something that gives you what you need, and that none of your team will ever find. Then you need to be gone."

Adrenaline courses through my veins, and a powerful mix of fear and excitement twist my stomach.

This is it. Time to focus, Marek. Everything hinges on the next few moments. Let's get this shit done.

"OK. I got it, Sully. In fact, I've had an idea," I say.

He turns to face me, and gestures for me to elaborate.

"They'll take the beta build, test it on their own hardware, right? They'll need to check its compatibility with their current setup. Hell, they install it on a stand-alone server that's in Wi-Fi range of their damn system, I can get in. So, I leave a little unlocked back door that's hidden to everyone but me, and that's how we get in."

"Unnoticed?" he asks.

I shrug.

"Yeah. Not for long, but I'll only need a minute or two to mine their data files. Then, boom. We find out whose funding this whole thing, and the exact details of the proposed virus. Boom. Down goes Mosner."

Sully nods decisively, and clicks his fingers.

"Right. Let's do this. When you're done here, go back to your place. I've got a business lunch I can cancel, and I'll come meet you. You can show me the info, and we can come up with a plan."

I smile at him, wanting nothing more than to feel his huge arms around me, squeezing me tight.

But that can wait.

"Go, Marek! Now!" Sully commands, and I jump to my feet, turning to leave as he picks up the receiver of his desk phone.

CHAPTER ELEVEN

MAREK

My heart is pounding in my chest as I hurry from Sully's office. The fear I'd felt at Sully's discovery of my plan had faded, only to be replaced with an anxious thrill of both excitement and panic.

I have to resist the urge to run as I head for the stairs, trying to keep my inner feelings from showing on my face. Carlos would already be on his way up to see Sully, likely already in the elevator as I skip down the first flight of stairs. It's a long way to the central floor, and I'm aware that time is of the essence.

If I don't get what I need to done within ten minutes of returning to my computer, then it's over. The whole thing will have been a failure. Sure, I could try and hack the system externally, but without a backdoor into the otherwise robust code, I'd be discovered in a matter of seconds by Monser's extremely skilled techs.

I've already written the segment of code I need to install. It's hidden away in an encrypted folder on my computer's hard drive - I couldn't risk having it on the server for fear of discovery. So, I just had to get back to my desk, and transfer the files over to the beta build.

Sully's words ring in my ears. I just have to hope he can stall Carlos for long enough for me to do what I have to do, and then get the hell out of here. The code would be all but invisible to anyone but me, so once it's installed - well, down goes Mosner. As long as I can hack a highly monitored and secure system in two minutes, with the only ally a simple Trojan Horse virus.

Easy.

I begin to feel more confident as my legs eat up the stairs, the exercise helping to burn off the adrenaline coursing through my veins. Before long I'm on my floor, and I take a few deep breaths to steady my heart rate before swinging the door open and striding out into the IT department.

Everyone is hard at work, focused intently on the screens in front of them, or talking on their phones in hushed and serious voices. I walk through barely unnoticed, and make my way to the secure hub at the center of the department.

"Hey, Marek," one of the guys says absently as I enter. "Everything OK? Carlos got called up by Sully a few minutes after you. He'll be back soon to go through your final report in a bit, I guess."

I don't respond for a moment, sitting myself down at my station and quickly logging in to the system.

"No," I respond. "I think I've fucked up. Bad. I need to check something real quick, but it's not looking good."

My fingers are a blur as I open up the Project Cutthroat beta build. My colleagues glance at me with concern, none choosing to respond to what I've said, or trying to work out exactly what I meant.

"Shit," the guy who'd spoken says. "That isn't good, man. Without you on the rectifications, we're going to be working twenty-four-seven for three days, probably over the weekend too."

His words earn a snort of amusement for another coworker.

"Hey, at least you can finally take your girl on that holiday she's been moaning about for a year. If not I could always take her for you, show her what a good time is."

The pair laugh, and I'm momentarily forgotten as they exchange good natured banter between them.

"Fuck off, Jim. Maybe I'll take your mom out for dinner when you're away. Give her just what she needs after - "

"Really?" I say, interrupting them. "Anyway, don't worry. You'll be fine. All the flaws are identified - Carlos can review my final report. I just missed a couple of things - thought I'd fixed them, but it seems I didn't do as good a job as I thought. Sully is *pissed*."

Most of the guys are back at work now, my made up plight pretty much forgotten.

"You'll be all right, Marek," a guy says. "You're a clever kid. I bet you'll get a new job in a few days, and this whole thing will be in the past. I got a bad feeling about this Project Cutthroat anyway. Why all this damn secrecy? What is Mosner trying to hide?"

If only I could tell you. You'd be walking out of here quicker than I can say deadly fast acting pathogen. But don't worry. I got this.

There's a few users logged in to the beta build editing suite, actively updating code, flagging areas that need attention and ticking off completed tasks. I open up a separate program - one I'd created myself that hides my activities in the editing suite. No one will even see that I'm logged on.

I glance at the clock in the bottom right of the screen. Five minutes left.

Come on, Marek.

I click open the encrypted folder containing my custom code, and type in a password to access the data. It's then a simple case of copying the long string of text, and transferring it over to the relevant section of the beta build.

I check no one is editing the area I'm putting it in before I copy it over. Luckily no-one is, or they might catch wind of the change. They wouldn't be able to make sense of the code, but they might realize something is up. Anyway, that doesn't matter. I'm clear.

The editing suite is live, with all data backed up every second in a separate server.

The only way anyone would notice the edit is if they checked every snapshot for the day, and spotted this erroneous change between two seconds. And no one was going to do that. It would take years.

Finally, I open up my final report and quickly update it to reflect the flaws I'd hidden from Carlos. Now my tracks are well and truly hidden.

My spirits lift as the update takes place, cemented into the core of the beta build. I clench my fists in triumph, resisting the urge to whoop with joy.

Instead, I act upset, rubbing a finger at an eye and shaking my head.

"Yeah. It's bad," I say forlornly. "I'm not coming back from this, guys."

I look over my shoulder. No sign of Carlos. But I only have one minute to get the hell out of dodge.

"I'm going to...I'm going. I think it's best I..." I pretend to choke, and pick up my few personal items from my desk and throw them into my backpack.

I rise to my feet, and take a deep, sobbing breath.

"I just need to get out of here. Get some air. I'll...good luck."

Everyone buys it. Faces look up at me, wide eyed and pitying. Suckers.

Hell, I could be an actor if this gig doesn't work out. I'd get an Emmy for that shit.

The room is deathly silent as I leave, with everyone stunned by what's happened. The further I get from the secure central hub, the more my confidence increases, and I allow myself a little smile as I head for the stairs.

It's a long way to the ground floor, but bumping into Carlos, or anyone for that matter, is the last thing I want right now.

I race down the flights of stairs, counting them as I go. I know Carlos will likely be on his way back to his desk now. Hopefully Sully told him that he'd fired me, asked me to go grab my stuff and leave. Which should tie up with what had just happened, as far as the rest of the team are concerned.

I feel a rush of excitement. Could this really be about to fall into place? I want to get home, to prepare for the next move.

None of this could have happened without Sully. If I hadn't fallen for him, Carlos would have fired me on the spot. He knew Sully and I had something going on, which is likely why he went to him first.

My cell phone buzzes in my handbag, and I take it out to see Sully's personal cell phone number calling me.

I click the line open and place the phone to my ear.

"If you're still at your desk, leave. Now," he says quickly in a low voice.

My laughter is met with a stunned silence.

"I'm just passing the fourth floor. I'm gone," I reply, smiling.

Sully breaths an audible sigh of relief.

"Good. Listen, Marek - Carlos doesn't suspect a thing. He bought what I told him. As long as you did what you needed to do, then we're good here. I have a few things to sort out over the next couple of days. I think it's best we don't talk, to avoid any suspicion."

His deep and masculine voice sends little shivers of pleasure down my neck and spine. With all the excitement that's happened, I suddenly find myself incredibly horny. An image of Sully's naked body enters my mind's eye, standing before me, aroused, with a hungry look in his eye.

"OK," I say. "I'll be waiting for you, Sully. I - "

I hesitate for a moment, wondering if what I'm about to say will be well received, or reciprocated even.

"I love you."

I reach the ground floor, and walk out into reception, and head for the exit.

"Sully?" I say, as the line goes silent.

"I love you too, Marek. Take care, all right? I've got to go," he replies, and the line goes dead.

A feeling of deep contentment fills me as I leave the building.

Now, time to prepare for Monday.

CHAPTER TWELVE

SULLY

I knock on the door to Marek's apartment. My arms are behind my back, hiding a bunch of deep red roses and a cold bottle of champagne. We haven't spoken since last week, when he'd left Fuller headquarters.

Today was the day when the beta build was due to go live on Mosner's systems. I'd personally handed over the files to their chief executive. Like me he's ex-military, or rather private contractor, who I knew back in the days of serving.

He's a shrewd, cruel man, rumored to have committed a number of horrendous crimes in the past, making my conviction to backup Marek's actions even stronger. After our meeting I'd plied him with expensive wine and cigars, and he'd opened up to me a little about their plans for testing.

The door slowly opens to reveal Marek, wearing a tight t-shirt and black boxer briefs. The outline of his cock is perfectly visible under the thin material of his shorts, distracting me momentarily.

"Are you just going to stare at my dick, or come in?" he asks with a coy smile.

I laugh at his words, taking another long look at his body.

"OK, I'm done," I say. "Here, I got you these."

I brandish the flowers and wine, feeling a little foolish at the cheesy gesture. But Marek smiles, his cheeks flushing a little.

"It's a bit early for champagne, isn't it?" he teases as he takes the gifts from me.

He steps into me and throws his arms around me. I hug him back, lifting him from his feet in a tight bear hug. He cries out in delight, and we simply stand there for a moment, Marek's warmth seeping through my clothes, his scent wafting over me.

I follow him into his apartment and close the door behind me. It's the first time I've been to his place, and I immediately feel at home with the comfy surroundings.

"That's for after. You know, when we've taken down Mosner," I say

My words seem surreal even as I speak them. I haven't told Marek yet, but I've arranged to step down as CEO of Fuller industries as soon as the news breaks. My most trusted of directors, a guy who'd served under me in Iraq, was ready to step in as interim CEO - the only guy who really knew what was about to go down. But I trusted him to keep his silence, and wait until the right moment to get things in action.

"I spoke to Mosner's CEO," I continue. "Cutthroat beta is going to go live on their systems in just under an hour. Are we ready?"

A thrill of excitement runs through me. Marek turns back to face me after placing the champagne in his fridge.

"Yup," he says simply. "Everything is prepared."

He takes me by the hand and leads me from the kitchen, back to the hall and then into a side room. His office.

I'm amazed at what I see. Four monitors, a number of base units glowing with green and blue LEDs. The computer, and various boxes dotted over the huge desk are all connected with a tangle of black cables.

"So, this is where the magic happens?" I say.

He stands up on tiptoes to kiss me gently on the lips.

"No, that's the bedroom," he whispers. "I'll show you that later…"

I feel a stirring of desire at his words, but try my best to suppress it for now. There will be plenty of time for that later.

The rest of our lives, in fact, if he really feels the same way about me as I do him.

He sits down in the plush leather armchair in front of his desk, and starts to tap away on the keyboard at an amazing speed. Various windows and applications appear on the monitors, and his eyes flick from one to another as his fingers move in a blur.

"I designed the code to alert me when it goes live," he says. "Then, I drop in a more complex virus, and boom. We're in."

I take up a seat next to him and observe him work in awe. I can't keep up with what he's doing as he works. I notice on one of the screens there's a list of jumbled numbers, letters and symbols that I recognize as code, though it makes no sense to me at all.

"What's that?" I ask, pointing at the screen.

"That's the software monitoring for a signal. It's telling me what's live and what's been shut down in all of the systems I'm monitoring."

He glances at me.

"I know it looks like jumbled nonsense to you, but to me, well, it's like a language. I can read it."

There's a loud ping from his speakers and a green section of code appears on his tracking software.

"Bingo," he says. "It's go time. Watch a master at work."

I decide to stay silent, not wanting to distract him from his work. He flicks his mouse over to the tracking software, and copies a section of code to a separate application.

"OK…" he says as he types furiously at the keyboard. "That's it. The Trojan should be live."

Marek flicks to his third monitor, and stares intensely at an application that seems identical to the tracking app. But there's no text, just a blank screen. Then, all of a sudden, it springs to live, lines upon lines of code streaming down the page.

Marek punches the air.

"That's it! It's worked! Now I can use this to…" his voice trails off as he concentrates, manipulating the software.

A screen pops up. Much the same as my desktop on my work laptop. A simple interface, with a number of hard drives listed on the screen.

"One minute thirty until they shut me down," he says quietly.

Then, he's opening the drives in turn, using a further app to carry out a search of the drives.

"Idiots," he says with a wry smile. "It's listed as Project Cutthroat on their own servers. Should have called in something else, at least made it hard for me."

I grunt in amusement. If these guys are anything, imaginative is definitely not one of them.

Marek lets out a loud breath and freezes as a number of windows open in turn on a monitor. He flicks between them briefly, his eyes wide.

"It's here, Sully. It's all here! Look!"

I follow his finger to see a vast number of documents and files. All related to the project. Financial spreadsheets, invoices, lists of payments and bank transfers.

Well, fuck. This is the jackpot.

I place a hand on Marek's shoulder and watch as he starts to copy the files over to his own system. The blue bar fills slowly, given the size of the data.

"Fuck," he says. "One minute. Come on, baby."

The bar is halfway with just over thirty seconds to go.

"The Trojan is going to annihilate itself in twenty seconds," he says as the bar continues to fill slowly.

I grit my teeth and pray. It can't end here, not now, we're so close.

Then, suddenly, the bar jumps, and fills to around ninety percent. After a few more seconds it fills, and the transfer window disappears.

Marek whoops with joy, and I cheer.

"We got it!" he exclaims. "Everything! And there was no sign of them even noticing."

I let out the breath I'd been holding for a long minute, the tension lifting from my shoulders. I'm shaking with adrenaline at how close we'd been to failure.

"That was something else," I say. "You're awesome, Marek."

He smiles a little shyly at me.

"It was nothing," he replies modestly. "And I couldn't have done it without you getting Carlos off my back."

I lean in to kiss him on the lips, and he moans in pleasure, his eyes half-closing for a moment.

"What now?" I ask.

He shrugs, his eyes on mine.

"We send this to multiple sources, all at the same time. It'll take them a while to work out what they're seeing, but after a couple of hours it'll hit the news. And then, Mosner's share prices plummet, and the government freezes their assets."

He winces.

"And, I guess Fuller will be hit hard too. Unless you drop the contract and distance yourself from all of this."

His eyes are wide, a slightly guilty expression on his face. I smile back, and he frowns.

"Don't worry about that. I've got a guy on the inside to handle it. Everything's in place, all I got to do is say the word."

He lets out a sigh of relief.

"Don't send it yet," I say.

Marek takes his hands from the keyboard and monitor, and looks at me quizzically.

"Let's go have some champagne. And then you need to pack some stuff," I tell him.

"Sully?" he asks. "What do you mean? Where are we going?"

I shrug, and then smile a broad, satisfied smile.

"Anywhere. My private jet is waiting for us at the airport. We can be out of the US before any of this hits the news," I reply.

He looks shocked, but a smile slowly spreads on his full lips.

"You're...you really mean it? What about your company? And - "

I shake my head and cut him off with a gesture.

"Like I said. All being handled. As of today, I'm no longer CEO of Fuller industries. I've stepped down after letting Project Cutthroat tarnish our name. But the company will bounce back. And I've diversified my investments to make my shareholding in Fuller meaningless."

Realization dawns on Marek, and he yelps in joy and jumps into my lap. I laugh, and hold him tight, and a feeling of deep joy and happiness spreads through me.

"Let's go somewhere hot," he says, his voice muffled with his face pressed into my chest. We both burst out into laughter, and I feel a sense of relief that this ordeal, and my old life, are both finally over.

EPILOGUE

SULLY

I'm reclining in a luxurious leather seat in my private jet, with Marek sitting to my left. Other than a stewardess and the piloting team, we're the only ones on board as the jet accelerates along the runway.

For the first time in forever, I'm nervous. I glance over at Marek, who's still in awe of his plush surroundings. I clink my champagne flute against his, and he smiles up at me happily.

"To us," I toast.

I take a long drink of the fizzy and fruity liquid to calm my nerves. I try to think of something to say to make small talk, but nothing comes to mind, so we sit in a comfortable silence as my jet takes off into the air.

Just before we left Marek's apartment, he distributed the information he'd hacked from Mosner. After reviewing a select few of the documents, especially the financials, we realized that the reality of Project Cutthroat was even worse than we thought.

The whole thing had been funded by a mysterious gray corporation, which didn't actually seem to exist when we looked into it. However, after a little sleuthing, we discovered where the money was actually coming from.

Russia. They were exploring alternatives to their costly nuclear weapons program in secret, and had settled on viral warfare after advice from Mosner's development team. With such a virus at their disposal, they would have become unstoppable, able to disable entire cities and countries within hours.

But that was all going to stop. We'd sent a copy of the entire data files to the US government, advising them to review it as a matter of urgency. It would be a matter of days until Mosner is taken down, meaning the Russians wouldn't get their hands on such a horrific weapon.

Marek had joked at the time that we'd saved the world. I'd simply replied that there's a good chance we probably have.

With the jet in the air, the stewardess comes over to pour us out some champagne, and to inform us of the in-flight schedule, with food being served a number of times during the flight. Marek quickly downs a second and then a third glass, much to my amusement.

I thank the stewardess, and tell her that once the first meal is served she should take a break in the crew quarters next to the cockpit, hinting gently that I'd like to be alone with Marek. I'd already told her what I'm planning, and she smiles at me knowingly as she heads off to the kitchen.

"This is amazing," Marek says. "I can't believe we left everything, just like that."

I take his hand in mine and give it a squeeze.

"It's good to get away," I respond. "Anyway, it's only temporary. Unwind and relax wherever we want for a few weeks, or months. Then we can go back. Or not."

I smile in satisfaction, the pressure of being CEO of a successful corporation finally starting to lift from my shoulders after years of hard work. The whole situation seems a little surreal, and I can scarcely believe what's happened over the few weeks that have passed in a whirlwind blur.

"Is everything alright? Is something bothering you?" I ask.

Marek shakes his head. He starts to say something, but decides against it, and his face flushes red.

I watch as Marek licks his luscious lips and crosses and uncrosses his legs several times. I wonder if he's uncomfortable. I wonder if he would not be far more comfortable if he was able to get out of those restrictive trousers...

"Did I tell you there's a bedroom at the back of the plane?" I ask quietly. "It's… secluded. Very private."

He giggles.

"Well, mister, why don't you show me?" he replies. "We've got to find some way to pass the time, after all."

I take his hand and pull him to his feet, and guide him along the corridor, past the kitchen, an office slash meeting room, a guest bedroom, and finally to the master suite. Marek opens the door, and his jaw drops at the sight of the luxurious bedroom.

I follow in behind him, closing the door and placing my hands on his hips. I turn him around to face me, and he drapes his arms around my shoulders.

He looks me in the eye for a moment, and smiles at an unspoken thought. I wonder at his expression, and what he's thinking about.

"Sully," he says softly. "Marry me."

I freeze. Everything suddenly falls into place. His panicky speed drinking when the flight attendant brought the champagne around. The multiple times he tried to say something then lost courage. His nervous fidgeting throughout the entire plane ride. Marek was trying to work up his courage.

I suddenly realize that I'm not saying anything, with Marek staring at me, expecting some sort of response. I slowly come back to reality, and it feels as though I'm slowly thawing.

"Marek?" he asks. "Are you OK?"

I pull him tight against me, and kiss the top of his head.

"Of course. Just a little shocked. You just caught me completely off guard, Marek," I say finally, as a mix of emotions churn in my stomach.

"I guess that means you want a little more time to think before you answer," Marek frowns.

"Oh, I've had plenty of time to think," I grin back. "You just derailed my plans a little bit."

Marek looks up at me. Now it's his turn to be shocked, and I chuckle at his look of confused amusement.

Then, I take a step back from him, and drop to one knee.

"I guess it's not too late for me to try to get things back on track," I say.

I reach into my pants pocket, grabbing a small jewelry box and opening it before brandishing it to Marek.

"Marek. I know we've not been together for long, but I've never been more certain about anything in my life than I have about my feelings for you. Will you marry me?"

He gasps in shock, holding a hand to his mouth.

"You're one upping me," he jokes after a moment. "I didn't bring rings." A tear of joy runs down his cheek.

"Yes! Of course I'll marry you," he adds with a smile.

I push the ring onto his left ring finger. It's a perfect fit. He studies the gleaming white metal and series of ones and zeros etched around the band signifying both of our first initials.

I stand and push him gently back, until he reaches the bed. He drops onto his butt, and pulls me on top of him, everything else forgotten as we tenderly share our love.

EPILOGUE

MAREK

M y stomach twists with nervous anticipation as I wait outside of the church hall. Time seems to slow as I wait for the wedding march to sound. My mom's arm is in mine, and I grip her tight for support.

The organ starts to play, and my mom guides me through the big wooden doors, and I look at the familiar faces around us as we head down the aisle.

I catch sight of Sully at the altar. He looks immaculate in his dark blue suit, his big hands clasped behind his back. He glances over his shoulder and smiles at me, showing no sign of nerves.

The mere sight of him puts me at ease. After the last few months of being at each other's sides, it's been a strangely tough day without his reassuring presence, and I long to feel his proximity once again.

I smile back at him, and then glance down around at my guests, still finding it a little strange that I'm now close personal friends with so many rich and important people. I can see doctors, CEOs, and even actors. We're actually getting married by a United States senator who served with Sully in Iraq.

Despite the butterflies in my stomach, I feel empowered and content with my decision. It just feels right, and to have Sully by my side, I know I can handle anything.

"Hey," he says simply as I take up my position beside him.

He shakes my mom's hand, and then places his arm around my waist and pulls me tight against him.

"You look amazing," Sully whispers in my ear, and the sound of his deep voice sends a tingle of pleasure through me.

"You aren't looking too bad yourself," I reply in a flash.

The ceremony passes in a blur, and I have no idea how much time has passed when we turn to leave, husband and husband. A cheer erupts in the room around us as we walk back down the aisle.

As we reach the door, our guests chant for us to kiss once again. Sully grins at me, and takes me into his arms. I yelp in surprise as he lifts me from my feet effortlessly, and plants a big kiss on my lips.

I drape my arms over his shoulders, smiling even as I kiss him, with shouts of encouragement coming from friends and family alike.

"Time to go celebrate, Mr. Williams-Fuller" he whispers in my ear.

I'm still in his arms as we walk from the old church, and head over to the huge pearlescent tent that's been erected in the center of the church ground's pristine lawn.

Sully's best man, Fuller Corp's new CEO, is suddenly at our side with his wife, and he beams at us.

"Congratulations, guys," he says.

Sully puts me down, and shakes his hand vigorously.

"Thanks," Sully says. "For everything. I needed to get away from all that. Find myself again. The company is in good hands."

He simply shrugs in response, as if it's no big deal. Fuller Corp's share price has bounced back since the exposition of the Mosner contract, and Fuller had expertly cancelled and distanced itself from the deal.

"Ain't no thing, boss," he says.

He glances over his shoulder at the approaching crowd.

"Listen. I didn't want to bring this up now, but I know you guys are outta here after the toasts."

We both look at Fuller's new CEO, wondering what he's going to suggest.

"I got approached by some shady dudes, looking for a way in. You should check out what they've been up to in the past. The whole thing stinks of Mosner, and the Russian deal."

He leans in to whisper at us.

"I can get you what you need. These guys are bad, I can feel it. My gut is telling me they're going to try and take us down."

Sully looks at me, and I nod back.

"We've got your back," he says. "These guys won't know what hit 'em. I'll call you in a week or so on a secure line. Keep them hanging until then, right?"

I smile contentedly. I knew I'd be using my skills again someday, and with Sully by my side? Anything is possible.

Talk of work is over as we're crowded by our guests, and ushered through with the moving group into the expansive marquee.

I see our two little flower girls -- Sully's nieces -- run by laughing and feel a twinge in my heart. I haven't brought it up yet, but I'm hoping that one day the future might hold a family for us. I glance up at Sully and notice he's watching the girls with a wistful look in his eye. It gets my hopes up even further.

Sully grips me tight and leads us to the head table, and I rest my head against his shoulder, feeling the happiest I've ever felt in my entire life.

Be the first to find out about all of Dillon Hart's new releases, book sales, and freebies by joining his VIP Mailing List. Join today and get a FREE book -- instantly! Join by clicking here!

ABOUT THE AUTHOR

Dillon Hart, who lives in San Francisco, writes compelling gay romance novels that embody the essence of love and human relationships. His works are inspired by the diverse communities that call the city home, from the vibrant Castro neighborhood to the bohemian Mission district. In his spare time, Dillon enjoys riding the F Line streetcar from Market Street to Fisherman's Wharf, where he enjoys the ocean breezes and the bustle of the waterfront.

More on www.dillonhart.com

Join my newsletter by clicking here.

Write me at contact@dillonhart.com

9 781088 119662